God Gave Us So Much

by Lisa Tawn Bergren ❖ art by Laura J. Bryant

WATERBROOK
PRESS

God Gave Us So Much
Published by WaterBrook Press
12265 Oracle Boulevard, Suite 200
Colorado Springs, Colorado 80921

ISBN 978-0-307-44629-9

Published in the United States by WaterBrook Multnomah, an imprint of the Crown Publishing Group, a division of Random House Inc., New York.

WaterBrook and its deer colophon are registered trademarks of Random House Inc.

Library of Congress Cataloging-in-Publication Data
Bergren, Lisa Tawn.
    God gave us the world / by Lisa Tawn Bergren ; [illustrations by Laura J. Bryant] — 1st ed.
        p. cm.
    Summary: While visiting a museum, Mama Bear tells Little Cub about all the different kinds of bears living around the world, and that God created this big, diverse planet to be their home.
    ISBN 978-1-4000-7448-8
    [1. Creation—Fiction. 2. Christian life—Fiction. 3. Polar bear—Fiction. 4. Bears—Fiction.] I. Bryant, Laura J., ill. II. Title.
    PZ7.B452233Gor 2011
    [E]—dc22
                                        2010011910
Bergren, Lisa Tawn.
    God gave us love / by Lisa Tawn Bergren ; art by Laura J. Bryant. — 1st ed.
        p. cm.
    Summary: Grampa Bear tells Little Cub all about God's love and why she should be patient, gentle, kind, and loving to family members and others, even when she does not like them very much.
    ISBN 978-1-4000-7447-1
    [1. Love—Fiction. 2. God—Love—Fiction. 3. Christian life—Fiction. 4. Polar bear—Fiction. 5. Bears—Fiction.] I. Bryant, Laura J., ill. II. Title.
    PZ7.B452233Gol 2009
    [E]—dc22
                                        2009004093
Bergren, Lisa Tawn.
    God gave us heaven / by Lisa Tawn Bergren ; art by Laura J. Bryant. — 1st ed.
        p. cm.
    Summary: Little Cub's father explains to her that God created heaven, the most wonderful place, because He loves us and never wants to be far from us.
    ISBN 978-1-4000-7446-4
    [1. Heaven—Fiction. 2. Christian life—Fiction. 3. Polar bear—Fiction. 4. Bears—Fiction.] I. Bryant, Laura J., ill. II. Title.
    PZ7.B452233Goh 2008
    [E]—dc22
                                        2007050522

Printed in the United States of America
2010—First Edition

10 9 8 7 6 5 4 3 2 1

God Gave Us the World

"What a beautiful world we live in!" Mama Bear said. "Just look at all this snow!"

Little Cub looked around. "We *always* have snow, Mama."

"Yes, but it's *always* different! Sometimes it's slushy, and sometimes dry, shimmering sparkles drifting from the sky. But this is my favorite kind of snow…big, fat flakes you can catch with your tongue!"

Little Cub giggled when she saw Mama trying to catch flakes on her tongue. "You look funny."

Mama smiled and nudged her with her hip. "You do too. I think you have the *pinkest* polar bear tongue I've *ever* seen."

"Ever?"

"Ever."

"Do all bears have pink tongues?"

"I don't know, Little Cub. God made a whole world full of bears. And we all look a little different."

"He did? Why'd he do that?"

"Because God is creative. Just like he made all kinds of places to live, he made all kinds of different bears… and all kinds of different bear tongues."

"Whoa, whoa, whoa!" Little Cub said.
"There are other kinds of places to *live*?"

"Well sure," Mama said.
"While the Pole is our home, lots
of bears live in far different places."

"Why would they wanna do that?"

BEAR
EXHIBIT

"Because they like their homes best. It's where God put them.
God gave us this great big, wide world and a whole bunch of
different bears with different fur and different families."

"Where do those other bears live? I've never seen 'em!"

"All around the world, Little Cub. Some very far from here."

"Panda bears live in China.
All they eat is bamboo."

"What's bamboo?"

"A kind of tree."

"They eat trees for *breakfast*?"

"Breakfast, lunch, and dinner!"

"And there are sloth bears in India.
They hang from trees and like to eat termites."

"Bugs? Eew!"

"They think they're delicious. And they have the
longest tongues you've ever seen!" Mama said.

GRIZZLY
BEARS

"Here we are. Grizzly bears live in America.
They like to catch fish."

"Phew!" Little Cub said. "Finally another bear who eats
normal food."

Mama smiled. "Even though other bears eat what you
might not like, we're all bears. God made us all.
God made the world and everything in it."

"Why not make us all the same?"

"We're not all the same on the inside, are we?

Some of us are quiet,

others LOUD!

Some of us like to move *fast*,

and others take their **t-i-m-e**.

I think it's fun that God made us
all bears, but all special too."

"Don't those other bears miss snow?" Little Cub asked.

"Do you miss the sand of the desert? Or the big green leaves of the rain forest? We love what we know, because it's *home* to us. Every bear has a special place in God's great, big world."

"Why not put us *all* here? Why not make us *all* polar bears?"

"Oh, there wouldn't be room here for all of us! And the world reflects God's work. How big, big, BIG he is. God can do *anything.* And if he's capable of anything, why would he make us *all* polar bears?"

"The whole world is like a mirror of God's work, Little Cub. Out of all the places he could've put us, he chose this world, Earth, to be our home. He made it just for us. God gave us this special world and every creature in it."

"Why'd he do that? Put us on
Earth, I mean."

"Because he is the Creator.
Can you imagine your Grandma
not cooking something new?
Or your Grampa not working on
a new birdhouse in his shop?

God created our world and everything in it, because it's in his nature to create. Understanding that is part of why he put us here…to serve and worship him, our amazing God, who gave us this amazing world."

"Do you 'member when he created it?"

Mama laughed. "Our world is older than anyone can remember. It's older than my great-grandmother's great-grandmother."

"Whoa, that's old. Like that huge ol' tree in the forest?"

"Older."

"It must be very strong."

"Very strong. And yet fragile too. We have to take care of our world. It's God's gift to us. He'd be sad if we hurt it."

"God might get mad if we hurt our world," Little Cub said. "I get mad when the twins hurt my stuff."

"Yes, I understand that," Mama said, picking her up. "We don't want to make God mad or sad. We want him to smile. We want to take care of this world he gave us."

"Do you think we'll ever meet the other bears?"

"Hmm. Maybe someday. It's a big world and constantly changing. It'd be fun to know more bears, wouldn't it?"

"Maybe a panda bear will come on an iceberg and bring us some bamboo!"

Mama laughed. "It's always good to make new friends, try new things, and know more about this world that God gave us."

Little Cub went to sleep that night, thinking about the stars in the sky and her special world.

She thought of other little bears falling to sleep, in forests and caves and jungles. And she was glad that God had made her, little her, to be one of the bears in it.

God Gave Us
Love

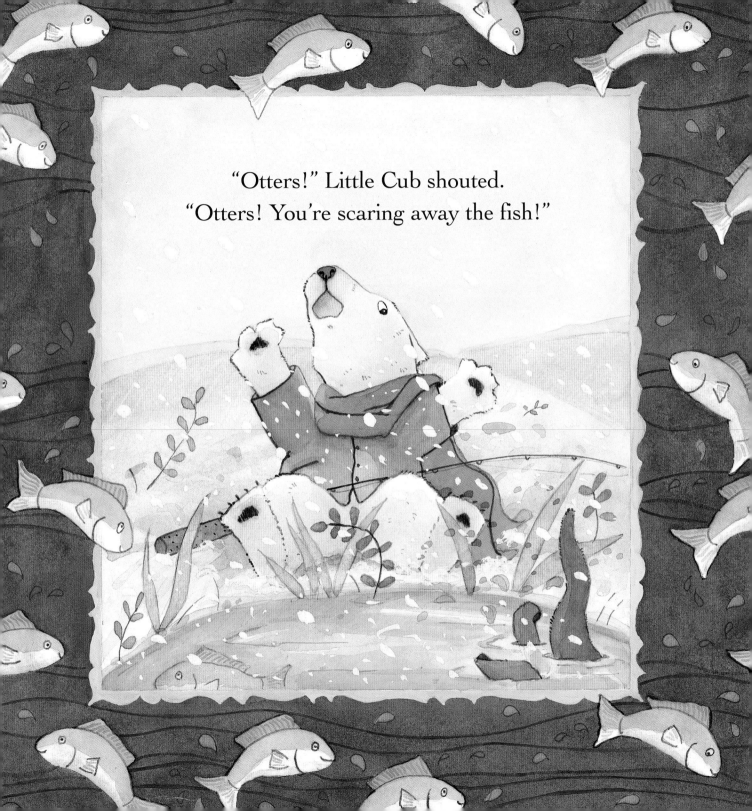

"Otters!" Little Cub shouted.
"Otters! You're scaring away the fish!"

"Easy, Little Cub," Grampa said. "The otters can share our spot."

"But Grampa," Little Cub complained, "if they scare all the fish away, we won't get any."

"That's all right," he said. "Half the fun of fishing is being together, right?"

"I...guess so."

"You know, Little Cub," Grampa said, "God wants us to show the otters love... He wants us to show everyone his love."

Little Cub thought on that awhile. "I love the otters. I just don't like them right now."

Grampa laughed. "I know *that* feeling."

"I always like *and* love you, Grampa,"
Little Cub said. "But why?"

"It's something deep within us,
something I can't totally explain—
only that God is love, so he created
us to love.
    He ties us all together like the
strings on our snowshoes, heart
to heart."

"I don't wanna love the otters like Mama and Papa love each other," Little Cub said. "You know, all that kissy and huggy stuff."

Grampa smiled. "The love between mamas and papas is a special kind of love, given by God. Someday you may even like it."

"God gave us love, all kinds of love.
The love of mamas and papas,
the love between friends and family.
And his love too."

"His love brings out the best in us, and families show us love all the time," Grandpa said.

"Group hug!" Little Cub yelled, and her sister and brother came running to join in.

They stood there for a bit.
It felt warm and cozy and *close*.

"I think *this* is God bringing out
the best in us," said Little Cub.
"I think this is God giving us love."

"Any time we show love,
Little Cub, we're sharing
a bit of his love."

"How come one minute I love these two and the next minute I feel like they're a couple of pesky otters?" Little Cub asked.

"Because while we *want* to love others as God loves us, we don't always *feel* like loving them. But when we choose to, it's always the right thing."

"God gave us love so we could see goodness in others, even when they make us grumpy."

"I know, I know," Little Cub said with a sigh. "God gave us love."

"Little Cub! God reminds us to show others love
by being patient, gentle, and kind," said Grampa.
"In all ways, we should try to show love."

"Oh," said Little Cub. "Right."

"Grampa, could we ever do something
to make God *not* love us?"

"Nope. He always hopes for the best in us.
He sees a bit of himself in us. And that bit is love."

"How do we *know* God loves us?"
Little Cub whispered.
"I mean, when we can't see or
touch or feel him?"

"We trust he's always with us,"
Grampa whispered back.
"Like your brother and sister
can't see you right now,
but they know you're here.
That's faith. God tells us he
loves us, and he shows us his love
over and over again."

"How does he show us his love?"

"He reaches out to us in a hundred ways and through those around us…and it gives us that same warm and cozy feeling."

"Like family?"

"And friends, and our home, or even food on our table," Grampa said. "Every which way he can, God shows us his love."

"Most of all," Grampa said, "we know God loves us because he sent his Son to save us, to show us the way. And to help us when we don't make good choices. Because God loved us that much, we will never ever be separated from him."

"Whoa," Little Cub said. "That's a lot."

"Yes, it is. That's a God-size love."

Little Cub fell asleep thanking God for loving her.

She asked him to help her love others better.

She thanked God for her grandparents and parents and
her friends and even the otters and her little brother and sister.

Because he had given her,
little her,
love.

God Gave Us Heaven

"Papa, what's heav'n?"

"Why, heaven is God's home…
the most amazing place we'll ever get to see."

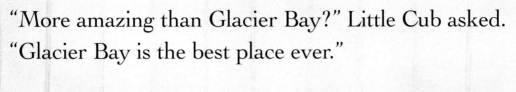

"More amazing than Glacier Bay?" Little Cub asked. "Glacier Bay is the best place ever."

"Yes, Little Cub. Even better than Glacier Bay."

"God has great plans for you, Little Cub."

"For me?"

"For you. Both here, and later, when we get to heaven.
God loves us and never wants to be far from us. He's made
a way for us to be with him forever, in heaven."

"When do we get to see heaven, Papa?"

"When our life here is over."

"When we die?"

"Yes, Little Cub, when we die."

"Will I be old like Grandma when I go to heaven?"

"I hope so, Little Cub. I hope you get to live a long and full life before you see heaven. But some of us get to see it sooner than others."

"They do? How come?"

"They get sick or something bad happens. But the good news is that no matter what bad things happen here, nothing bad happens in heaven!"

"Nothing bad at all?"

"No more tears, no more sadness, no more pain.
Only good. Only smiles!"

Little Cub thought on that for a while. "Will we eat in heaven?"

"Will we eat? Will we eat! We'll have more food than we need!
It'll be the best of all polar bear feasts!"

"Every day?"

"Every single day."

"What else will we do in heaven?"

"Worship God and explore the best place we've ever seen."

"Will we get bored of that?"

"I doubt it. Heaven will be a million times better than even this!"

"Can we take our stuff to heaven?"

"No, we won't need our stuff there, Little Cub." He paused and lifted her backpack from her shoulders. "Feel how heavy that is? Doesn't it feel good to have it off of you?"

Little Cub nodded.

"Sometimes we think we need stuff, but it's just more weight for us to carry. Our best stuff doesn't weigh anything at all— stuff like love,

        family,

                friends,

                     and faith.

That's where our real blessings are."

"What will God look like, Papa?"

"Hmm…you know what Mama looks like?
How she looks like love to us?
God will be like that…"

"'Cept a hundred times better!"

"Exactly."

"Will we be angels?"

"No. Only angels are angels. God made us polar bears for a reason."

"Shoot. I wanted to fly."

Papa laughed. "Me too. But you never know what we'll get to do in heaven. I bet we'll think it's even better than flying."

"Will I get to see you in heaven?"

"I think so, Little Cub. I think we'll see all our loved ones there. It will be like the best family reunion ever."

"How do we get there, Papa? To heaven, I mean."

"Hmm… Let's say this side of the canyon is life here, on earth.
And that side over there—where we find the path home—is heaven.

God knew that our bad choices might keep us from him forever. Might even wash us away! He didn't want that. He loves us too much."

"So he sent his very own Son, Jesus, to be our bridge. All we have to do is walk across it to head toward our forever home."

Little Cub thought on that. "I like Jesus," she said.

"So do I, Little Cub. So do I."

"Will I have a room in heaven?"

"Oh yes, there will be many rooms in heaven."

"Will it be as cozy as mine?"

"The coziest ever, Little Cub."

"Will I sleep in heaven?" she said with a yawn.
It had been a very big day. Papa yawned too and they
giggled together.

"Heaven will be full of all the things we love most,"
Papa said. "And right now, sleep sounds heavenly to me."

Little Cub went to sleep and dreamed of seeing
God and his angels, of singing and smiling
all day long. Of her best friends
and her whole family being
with her forever.
Of playing,
of laughing,
of everything good.

And she was glad, so glad, that
God had given them all
heaven.

LISA TAWN BERGREN is the award-winning author of nearly thirty titles, totaling more than 1.5 million books in print. She writes in a broad range of genres, from adult fiction to devotional. She makes her home in Colorado, with her husband, Tim, and their children, Olivia, Emma, and Jack.

LAURA J. BRYANT studied painting, printmaking, and sculpture at the Maryland Institute College of Art in Baltimore. She has illustrated numerous award-winning children's books, including *God Gave Us You, Smudge Bunny,* and *If You Were My Baby.* Laura lives in Asheville, North Carolina.

Also Available:

ISBN: 978-1-57856-323-4

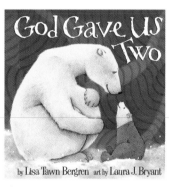

ISBN: 978-1-57856-507-8

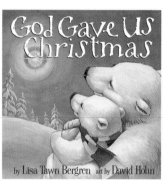

ISBN: 978-1-4000-7175-3

Over one million copies in the series sold!